MARLENE MARLOWE INVESTIGATES

THE GREAT CHRISTMAS PUDDING MYSTERY

I ran over and pushed open the door. Inside, a dreadful sight confronted me. A trail of dark red, sticky mess led across the bakery floor to a bundle in the furthest corner of the room. It looked like a sack of potatoes. But then it started to shiver and mumble. I looked at it again. And then I looked away. There was no doubt about it. The bundle was Aunt Maud.

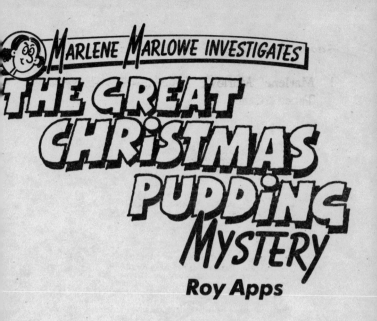

MARLENE MARLOWE INVESTIGATES
THE GREAT CHRISTMAS PUDDING MYSTERY

Roy Apps

Illustrated by David Farris

Hippo Books
Scholastic Publications Limited
London

Scholastic Publications Ltd.,
10 Earlham Street, London WC2H 9RX, UK

Scholastic Inc.,
730 Broadway, New York, NY 10003, USA

Scholastic Tab Publications Ltd.,
123 Newkirk Road, Richmond Hill,
Ontario L4C 3G5, Canada

Ashton Scholastic Pty. Ltd.,
P O Box 579, Gosford, New South Wales,
Australia

Ashton Scholastic Ltd.,
165 Marua Road, Panmure, Auckland 6,
New Zealand

First published by Scholastic Publications Limited, 1989
Text copyright © Roy Apps, 1989
Illustrations copyright © David Farris, 1989

ISBN 0 590 76088 2

Made and printed by Cox and Wyman Ltd.,
Reading, Berks

Typeset in Plantin by COLLAGE (Design in Print)
Longfield Hill, Kent

**Marlene Marlowe Investigates
the Great Christmas Pudding Mystery**
first appeared as a five-part serial on BBC School Radio;
performed by Anne Rosenfeld
and produced by Eleri Jones.

PUDDLETHORPE POLICE CENTRAL COMPUTER

FILE 1.1: LICENSED PRIVATE DETECTIVES

NAME: MARLENE MARLOWE

LICENCE NO: 1 BIGTWIT

ADDRESS: FLAT 222 PUDDLETHORPE POINT,
PUDDLETHORPE-ON-SEA

TELEPHONE: PUDDLETHORPE 998

PROFESSIONAL STATUS Claims she has handled more cases than any other Private Eye in Puddlethorpe.
This could well be true as she used to be a porter at Waterloo Station.

FEES: Most clients pay £5 for her to visit
— and £500 for her to go away

CHAPTER 1

It all began late on a wintry November evening. Outside the streets were bathed in a thick, chill fog, but I awoke with a start from an uncomfortable doze to find that my whole body ached and was hot, sticky and sweaty. My mouth tasted like a lump of second-hand chewing-gum that's been stuck on a school desk for a week.

I looked round about me. A bright, white light shone down into my face. In desperation I tried to recall what had happened. Then a strange smell of burning filled my nostrils and suddenly I remembered. I'd fallen asleep in my clothes again!

On the sun-bed!!

And the end of my nose was alight!!!

I leapt up, ran to the bathroom and plunged my head into a basin of water. There was a sizzling sound as the cold water began to put out the fire on my nose. It was then I heard a strange sound coming from the direction of the bathroom cabinet.

1

"Peep, peep. Peep, peep."

My Private Detective's instinct told me that it could only be one thing: a mouse with hiccups. Still with my head in the basin of water, I felt upwards with my right hand and flung open the door of the bathroom cabinet. Carefully and quietly I felt round for my toothbrush, toothpaste and extra large jar of Biffo the Bear Bubble Bath, trying to grab hold of the mouse. I could still hear it hiccupping:

"Peep, peep. Peep, peep."

This mouse was obviously trying to make me look stupid. In fact, I thought, it might well be a Taking-the-Mickey Mouse. Then, suddenly, my hands felt something. It was large and smooth. It had buttons all the way down it's front. There was no doubt about it, this mouse was wearing a shirt. Carefully I picked it up. It stopped going "peep, peep". I'd just taken my head out of the wash-basin to have a look when to my horror it started trying to talk to me!

"Hello! Hello!"

And I looked at what I was holding on to in my shaking hand and realized it was my Supa Slim-Style De Luxe Cellular Car Phone. Special because it's the only car phone in existence that can disguise itself as a mouse. Quickly, I placed it to my ear.

The voice on the other end spoke again. It sounded strangely familiar.

"Hello! Is anybody there?"

MARLENE MARLOWE'S GUIDE FOR PRIVATE DETECTIVES

1: TELEPHONES

Always keep your car phone in the bathroom — it will save you having to go out to the car to answer it if you are cleaning your teeth.

PEEP PEEP PEEP PEEP

The voice enquired again in a more urgent and chilling tone:

"I said, is there anybody there!"

I stood quite still. Slowly, I turned my head and looked over my left shoulder. The shower cubicle was empty. Then I looked over my right shoulder; apart from my yellow rubber duck, its head stuck firmly down the plug-hole, the bath was empty too.

"No. There's no one here," I whispered.

"Eh? Well, of course there's somebody there," the voice on the phone was getting tetchy.

"But — I've looked and—"

Suddenly the voice boomed down the phone like a

frantic foghorn:

"Well *you're* there, aren't you, Marlene Marlowe, answering the phone? You pea-brained nincompoop!"

A cold shiver ran down my spine. Then it ran all the way down the back of my legs to the tips of my toes. Then it ran all the way up again. Now I knew who was on the other end of the phone. Only three things send a cold shiver like that down my spine: someone putting ice cubes down my back, little green men from Mars and my Aunt Maud.

"Aunt Maud. Is that you?"

"Well, who do you think it is?"

I thought hard. "A little green man from Mars?"

I caught the scent of a whiff of smoke coming out of the car phone. There was no doubt about it, Aunt Maud was fuming.

"Do I sound like a little green man from Mars?" she roared.

"No," I admitted, "but you do sometimes *look* like a little green man from Mars, particularly after you've had a triple helping of chocolate fudge ice-cream."

"Marlene!" Aunt Maud's voice boomed so that the car phone shook in my hand. "Just button your lip and listen! The pips are about to go!"

"Are they? Where are they going to go to?" I asked. But Aunt Maud could not — or would not — say.

"Marlene. Just get round here straight away!"

"Right on, Auntie, I'm on my way," I said, with some difficulty. Well, it's not easy to speak when your lip is buttoned. I was about to put the car phone back with the bubble bath when I heard:

"MARLENE!"

"Auntie?"

"Marlene, you dithering dumpling! You haven't asked me where I am."

"Oh. All right. Where are you, Auntie?"

"You know the evil torturer's cell in the Hangman's Dungeon underneath the haunted Castle?"

I paused and felt myself swallowing hard. "Y-y-y-es," I stammered.

"Well, I'm not there. I'm somewhere even more eerie and frightening." There was a nervous edge to Aunt Maud's voice. "I'm at Peregrine Postlethwaite's Bakery."

"Peregrine Postlethwaite's Bakery isn't eerie and frightening, Auntie."

"It is with all these glazed eyes with their blank stares watching my every move."

"Glazed eyes . . . ?"

"Yes. Twelve trays of gingerbread men right in front of my nose. But Marlene, listen. Something awful's happened." She paused before blurting out the dreadful words. "Peregrine Postlethwaite's Prize Christmas Pudding has disappeared!"

"You haven't eaten it, Auntie?"

"No, I haven't eaten it, you heartless half-wit! It's been stolen! Now get over here quick."

"Yes, Auntie."

"And Marlene . . . " The tone of her voice was strict and I knew exactly what she was going to say.

"Your balaclava."

"Oh, Auntie . . . You don't want me to put on my pink, woolly balaclava, do you?"

"Of course not, Marlene. Don't be silly."

"Well, thank goodness for that—"

"I want you to put on your new purple and orange, woolly balaclava."

"But Auntie!"

"It's a cold night, Marlene. And besides, I knitted it especially for you."

"Yes Auntie."

"Oh, and Marlene—"

"Yes Auntie?"

"Just be careful out there. The people involved in this little racket are capable of — of anything. That's why it has to be a case for Puddlethorpe's greatest Private Detective."

"And who's that, Auntie?"

"You, Marlene Marlowe, you blithering buffoon!" And with that, the pips went and the phone was dead.

I thought, buffoon. I had been called many things, but never a buffoon. I wondered what it meant. I took down my battered copy of *The Very Concise Dictionary for Private Detectives* and looked up "buffoon". This is what it said:

Buffoon (n):   twit.

So now I knew.

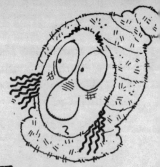

CHAPTER 2

I slipped on my baggy burgundy pants. Then I slipped on my bright blue blazer, my brilliant fluorescent black braces, my big brown boots and my purple and orange balaclava. Then I slipped on a bar of soap and slid out of the bathroom on my backside.

"Wheeeeeeeeee!!!!!!!"

In no time at all — well, two minutes and thirteen seconds to be exact — I'd slid all the way down the stairs, into the garage and on to the

Wheeeeeeeeeeeee

driving seat of my car, the famous Marlenemobile Mark One-And-A-Quarter . . .

I pulled my new purple and orange woolly balaclava over my head.

Oooohhhh!!!!

It squashed my wet hair down, squeezing out the water so that it ran all down my face, my neck, my back, my legs and into my boots.

But something was wrong! Although I had my foot hard down on the accelerator, the car was hardly moving. There was only one thing for it. I found the ignition key and turned it. The engine roared into life. Some cars purr like a tiger, other cars roar like a lion; the Marlenemobile croaks like a crocodile chewing a set of spanners.

I crashed the Marlenemobile into gear, then I crashed it into the garage wall, the front door and the

garden gate, before I finally hit the road.

And the road hit me back.

In no time at all, I was careering through the streets of Puddlethorpe-on-Sea at top speed — fifteen miles an hour.

MARLENE MARLOWE'S GUIDE FOR PRIVATE DETECTIVES

2: CARS

A decent car is vital for private detective work. Every Private Detective's car should have the following:

1: Three wheels — a Spare Wheel in the back for emergencies, a Steering Wheel in the front for steering and a Wagon Wheel in the glove pocket for tea breaks.

2: A large boot — so you can hop across muddy fields without getting your foot wet.

3: A sign in the back window saying KEEP YOUR DISTANCE! so that any villains giving chase don't get too close.

The night was silent and very, very dark. I checked my special Private Detective's Shock-Resistant, Water-Repellent, All-Digital Quartz Chronometer and Wrist Watch. The big hand was on Noddy and the little hand was on Big Ears. My heart missed a beat: it was later than I'd realized.

I swung the Marlenemobile off the main road and into a squalid part of town, where the streetlights were all broken and old coke cans rolled about in the gutter. A couple of old mangy mongrels trotted past me on the pavement. Yes, this was the kind of area where even the stray dogs walked around in pairs.

Then, looming up out of the darkness, I made out the sombre shape of a huge building. Above it was a large neon-lit sign that read:

PEREGRINE POSTLETHWAITE, BAKER
PURVEYOR OF THE MOST PERFECT PASTRY,
PUDDINGS AND PROFITEROLES IN PUDDLETHORPE

My Private Detective's training told me that this sign could mean only one thing — this was the bakery belonging to Peregrine Postlethwaite, Purveyor of the Most Perfect Pastry, Puddings and Profiteroles in Puddlethorpe.

I got out of the Marlenemobile and strolled over to the large, foreboding building. The chill, damp mist still hung about the deserted streets. I stood perfectly still and listened. I could hear nothing. There was no alternative: I rolled my purple and orange woolly balaclava up over my ears.

The sound of a seagull's high-pitched squawking hit me immediately. Then I suddenly realized it

wasn't a seagull that was squawking, but an old crow. And not any old crow, but a very particular old crow indeed — my Aunt Maud.

"Aunt Maud!" I called.

Aaarrrwwww!

Her pitiful shrieks were coming from somewhere inside the awesome bakery building. I ran over and pushed open the door. Inside, a dreadful sight confronted me. A trail of dark red, sticky mess led across the bakery floor to a bundle in the furthest corner of the room. It looked like a sack of potatoes. But then it started to shiver and mumble. I looked at it again. And then I looked away. There was no doubt about it. The bundle was Aunt Maud.

CHAPTER 3

Slowly and gingerly, I picked my way through the pools of thick, red, sticky blood and knelt down beside Aunt Maud. I looked again at her crumpled figure and froze on the spot. Brrrr! I knew I should've worn my thermal vest.

I bent over her and whispered into her ear.

"   !   ?"

It was no good. I was speaking so quietly, I couldn't even hear myself speak. I tried again, louder.

"Aunt . . . ! Aunt Maud . . . ?"

A strange smile spread about her lips.

"Oh Henry! Oh you naughty thing, you'll smudge my lipstick!" she said.

"Auntie . . . ?"

"Eh . . . ? What . . . ?" She sat up with a start. Then she sat down with a finish. She looked hard at my face and let out a terrible scream: "Eiiihhhh!!"

"Auntie! It's me! Marlene-Marlowe-Private-Detective-Your-Niece!"

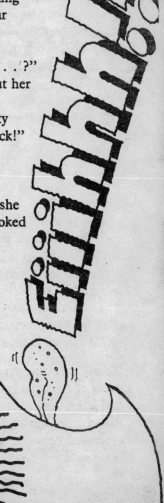

"Marlene? Is it really you? Your face — it's all orange and purple stripes. You gave me such a fright."

"Sorry, Auntie. Only I got my head wet putting out my nose and it made the orange and purple dye in my new balaclava run all down my face."

"Honestly, Marlene, what did you have to go and wake me up for? I was having such a lovely dream . . . such a lovely dream."

"Are you sure you're all right, Aunt Maud?

"All right?"

"Or shall I call you a doctor?"

"You can call me what you blessed well like, so long as it isn't rude," Aunt Maud grunted.

"But — aren't you injured . . . " I stammered. "I mean the trail of blood—"

"Injured? I was having forty winks, that's all."

"Forty winks? I don't believe it," I said.

"No, you're right, Marlene. That's not quite the truth. By the time you got here, I'd had more like four *hundred* winks."

"But, Auntie, the trail of blood . . . you must have had a shock."

"The only shock I've had was seeing your face, Marlene. Mind you, come to think of it, orange and purple stripes don't half improve the look of it."

"But who's responsible for all this?" I asked, surveying the bloody mess.

"Oh, some fellow."

"What fellow?"

"Stringfellow. Stomper Stringfellow to be precise. And his gang. I saw them off, of course. Well, there were only about thirty-three of them."

"Did they have guns and knives?" I asked.

"Worse than that."

"Worse?"

Aunt Maud stared me full in the face and whispered into my ear. "They had jam doughnuts."

Jam doughnuts! That explained everything.

"Oh, so this red, sticky stuff that's splashed about the room isn't blood, after all — it's strawberry jam!" I laughed and put my finger in some and licked it. "Mmmm . . . "

Aunt Maud caught her breath. "Well . . . actually, that bit of sticky stuff you've just licked off your finger isn't."

"Isn't?"

"Isn't strawberry jam."

I suddenly felt very sick. Very sick indeed.

"No," continued Aunt Maud. "That bit's raspberry jam. Can't you see the pips?" Aunt Maud dipped her fingers in, too.

"Mmmm, very tasty. But that's enough of that."

Aunt Maud stood up, did three knee-bends, touched her toes four times, and then adjusted the bottom row of her false teeth.

"Right!" she said. "Let's get after Peregrine Postlethwaite's Prize Christmas Pudding." Already Aunt Maud was at the door to the Old Bakery and on her way out to where the Marlenemobile stood waiting.

"Auntie," I called after her, "you mean you know where the Christmas Pudding is?"

"Of course I do! It's with Peregrine

Postlethwaite!"

"What! You never told me they'd kidnapped Peregrine too!" I exclaimed. But Aunt Maud couldn't hear me; she was already in the Marlenemobile, tooting the horn. Her 250-megawatt voice echoed across the derelict wasteland, drowning the sound of the car horn.

"C-O-M-E A-L-O-N-G M-A-R-L-E-N-E!!! Y-O-U D-I-T-H-E-R-I-N-G D-O-L-T-H-E-A-D!!!!!" she boomed. And twelve panes of glass in the bakery's windows shattered in sympathy.

CHAPTER 4

I ran to the Marlenemobile and jumped into the driver's seat.

"What! You never told me they'd kidnapped Peregrine too!" I expostulated again.

"That's by the by," Aunt Maud tossed her head. "Getting the Prize Christmas Pudding back is the important thing!"

"Auntie! How could you be so heartless!" I said. I was shocked by her callousness.

"Heartless?" Aunt Maud snorted. "Peregrine Postlethwaite's old enough and ugly enough to look after himself."

"But Stomper Stringfellow is one of the most gory and gruesome gangsters in Puddlethorpe—"

"And one of the most greedy," interrupted Aunt Maud. "Listen, Marlene. Postlethwaite's Prize Christmas Puddings are the richest, tastiest, fruitiest, weightiest Christmas Puddings in the land. Tell me this, Marlene, what would you rather have with a delicious dollop of custard for *your* Christmas dinner — a slice of Peregrine Postlethwaite, or a slice of Peregrine Postlethwaite's Prize Christmas Pudding?"

I thought. Then I thought again. Aunt Maud certainly had a point.

I started the Marlenemobile and we sped off along the dark, deserted streets towards . . . towards . . . er . . .

Suddenly I realized—

"Auntie, where are we going?"

"Goodness knows, Marlene. You're doing the driving."

There was screech of tyres as I brought the Marlenemobile to a halt. There was only one way to find out where we were going. I took out my *Private Detective's C★O★M★P★U★T★E★R★F★A★X File* from the glove compartment. If I had the address of Stomper Stringfellow's hideout on the printout then we stood a good chance of recapturing the pudding and Peregrine — and of discovering what Stomper Stringfellow's evil intentions were. I looked up the one headed "R" for *Really Evil Villains* and found the entry for "Stomper Stringfellow". This is what it said:

R

Really Evil Villains

STOMPER STRINGFELLOW:

REAL NAME:	Fred Stringfellow
HEIGHT:	190 centimetres
WEIGHT:	122000 grams
EYES:	Two
NOSE:	Broken
FAVOURITE COLOUR:	Slime green
MOST FAVOURITE FOOD:	Lightly grilled frog's spawn
LEAST FAVOURITE FOOD:	Christmas Pudding
PERSON HE MOST ADMIRES:	Count Dracula
ADDRESS OF HIDEOUT:	Not known

"Heck!"
I exclaimed.
"According to this
C★O★M★P★U★T★E★R★F★A★X
printout Stomper
Stringfellow hates Christmas
Pudding."

"Then he's not only a villain. He's a
buffoon." ★

I smiled. I knew what that meant.
"But Auntie, don't you see? If he hates
Christmas Pudding, why should he go
to all the trouble of stealing Peregrine
Postlethwaite's Prize example?"

"If you just stop your blessed prattling
and get us to his hideout, perhaps we
can find some answers!" Aunt Maud
muttered grumpily. "And some
pudding," she added, smacking her lips.

I looked at the C★O★M★P★U★T★E★R★F★A★X
again. The address of Stomper Stringfellow's
hideout wasn't on it.

"Er . . . " I said sheepishly. "I'm afraid I can't
tell you the address of Stomper Stringfellow's
hideout."

"No? Well, I know where they've gone," said Aunt
Maud.

"You do? Then why didn't you say so in the first
place?"

"You didn't ask," Aunt Maud reasoned. "You see,
I heard them talking. They've taken that delicious,

★ SEE PAGE 7

scrumptious Prize Christmas Pudding—"

"And Peregrine," I added.

"Oh, and him — to some people called Nasium."

"Nasium? Funny sort of name."

"John and Jim Nasium."

The name sounded familiar. John and Jim Nasium . . . Nasium . . . Where had I heard it before? Of course! Suddenly the penny dropped. Aunt Maud picked it up and put it in her handbag.

"Oh! You mean John's Gymnasium," I said.

"Yes! Jim's Johnasium. That's the place," exclaimed Aunt Maud triumphantly. "Its's in an old, converted warehouse down by the shore."

"Then we're facing in the wrong direction, Auntie!" I immediately slammed the Marlenemobile into reverse and Aunt Maud's false teeth immediately slammed into the dashboard. Quickly I turned the Marlenemobile round and headed off back the way we'd come.

"Right. Tell us the whole story, Auntie," I said. "About the doughnut fight at Peregrine Postlethwaite's bakery. And how you got into that dreadful jam — and into that strawberry jam, too."

Aunt Maud sat back and took a deep breath. "Gish. Lell ush fig . . . " she began.

"But put your false teeth back in your mouth first," I added quickly.

23

CHAPTER 5

Aunt Maud put her teeth back in, sat back and took another deep breath.

"I'd just popped into Peregrine Postlethwaite's to get two dozen Viennese whirls, ten custard tarts and six chocolate eclairs—"

"Two dozen Viennese whirls, ten custard tarts and six chocolate eclairs?" I queried.

"My supper. Don't interrupt, Marlene. Anyway, all of a sudden the door banged open and Stomper Stringfellow's ugly looking gang burst in, followed by Stomper Stringfellow himself. 'Hold it there, everyone!' he threatened. 'This doughnut's got jam in it. If anyone moves, they'll come to a sticky end.' No one moved. 'Postlethwaite!' Peregrine stepped forward. His face was deathly white. That was because he had his head in a bowl of flour. 'Go on,' he whined. 'Do your worst. The money's in the safe, the antiques are in the cupboard and my stamp collection's under the pillow.' Stomper Stringfellow sneered at him. 'I don't want your money, Postlethwaite. Or your antiques or your stamps. I want that Christmas Pudding.' 'No . . . no . . . anything but that,' pleaded the wretched Postlethwaite. Oh, he's such a puny specimen! I was getting bored. 'Look, while you're waiting for the pudding, how about a bit of French stick for starters,' I volunteered, and whacked Stringfellow round the back of the knees with a baguette. And with that the doughnuts started flying about and

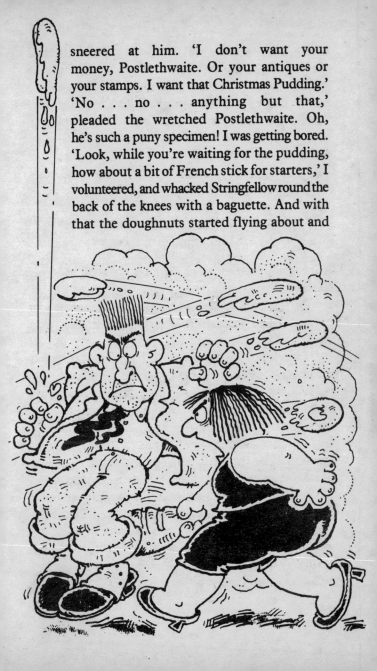

before I knew what was happening Peregrine had got one right on the end of his nose. He was so surprised, the Christmas Pudding flew out of his hands and he fell flat on his face. Then Stomper Stringfellow caught the pudding in one hand and dragged Peregrine off in the other and, as I started to give chase, I slipped up on a mouldy currant loaf and landed with my legs in the air. Then I got up and rang you, Marlene."

"Is that all?" I asked.

"Yes," said Aunt Maud.

"Well, that wasn't a very long story."

"This isn't a very long chapter," explained Aunt Maud.

"But what does Stomper String-fellow want with a Prize Christmas Pudding, if puddings are his least favourite food?"

Aunt Maud shrugged.

"What I can't understand," she said, "is why on earth they bothered to kidnap Peregrine Postlethwaite. He may well be the purveyor of the most perfect pastry, puddings and profiteroles in Puddlethorpe, but he's a snivelling, whining, little creep. Two minutes in his company is like your driving, Marlene."

"Like my driving? What do you mean, Auntie?"

"It sends you up the wall."

Quickly, I drove the Marlenemobile back down the wall.

We had reached the riverside. I stopped the

engine and turned off the lights. The old warehouse that was John's Gymnasium lay just ahead of us along the tow path.

"I hope they've been gentle," Aunt Maud said.

"So do I. If Peregrine's as weedy as you suggest."

"I meant with the Christmas Pudding!" Aunt Maud exclaimed in exasperation. She dabbed the tip of her nose with her face powder one last time, and slipped her compact back into her handbag. Then she took a lump of chewing-gum out of the glove compartment, rolled it round in the palm of her hand and popped it into her mouth. She turned to look me straight in the eye.

"O.K. Let's go," she said.

CHAPTER 6

Quietly, I opened the door of the Marlenemobile and let Aunt Maud out. It was still a dry and clear night.

"Ooooh, Marlene!" I heard Aunt Maud saying. "It's soaking wet out here."

I realized that this could mean only one of two things: either the weather had changed dramatically in the last three seconds and it was raining heavily — or Aunt Maud was taking a midnight dip in the river.

"Marlene, you dim-witted dimbo!" I could hear Aunt Maud's gurgling cries. "Help me out of this blessed river!"

I rushed to the water's edge and pulled out a dripping Aunt Maud. "Auntie, if you wanted a

swim, you should've said and I would've lent you my flippers and snorkel—"

"You mindless, muddle-brained mop-head!" I looked round. No-one was about. There was no doubt about it — Aunt Maud was talking to me.

"You parked the Marlenemobile so the passenger door opened out straight into the river."

"Oh, I'm sorry Aunt—"

"Sorry . . . A-a-a-tchoo!!!"

"Oh, Auntie, you won't catch pneumonia, will you?"

"Of course not. People of my age only catch *old* monia."

I made Aunt Maud sit on the Marlenemobile's radiator for a bit and in no time at all she was dry.

We crept along the towpath towards the old warehouse that was John's Gymnasium. There was little sound, save the lapping of the water on the riverbank and the occasional "ATCHOO!!!" from Aunt Maud. We stopped in front of the dark, windowless building.

"Here we are then," whispered Aunt Maud. "Jim's Johnasium."

"No, Auntie, John's Gym . . . " My voice trailed off as I looked above the door to where the light from the moon picked out the letters:

J I M ' S   J O H N A S I U M

I looked, and then looked again, hardly able to believe my eyes.

"But . . . what is Jim's Johnasium?" I asked Aunt Maud.

"Jim's Johnasium? It's a spoonerism, of course."

"Oh," I said. "Of course! Silly me!"

While Aunt Maud polished her spectacles in readiness for our assault on Jim's Johnasium, I quickly looked up "spoonerism" in my copy of *The Very Concise Dictionary for Private Detectives*. This is what it said:

---

spoonerism (n): the muddling up of the bront and facks of two or more words.

"Yes," Aunt Maud was saying, "John's always had trouble getting the letters of his words in the right order."

The sign above the bell said

REASE PLING

but as our weapon was surprise we ignored it and turned the handle of the old door. It creaked as we gingerly pushed it open. We were in a long, dark corridor at the end of which were a pair of swing doors with large windows, through which bright lights were shining.

On the other side of the windows we could see all kinds of equipment. There were weights, punch-balls, wall bars, and a trampoline . . .

"There he is!" I cried to Aunt Maud, as I spotted Peregrine Postlethwaite on the trampoline with three ugly looking brutes.

"You take Peregrine, I'll take the pudding. Let's get stuck in!" said Aunt Maud.

"Hold it!" I whispered. I'd caught a glimpse of Stomper Stringfellow himself. He was six feet tall and three feet wide. He had the kind of haircut you'd expect to find on a lavatory brush. He was beating a solid leather punch-ball with his bare fists. I imagined what it would be like if that punch-ball had been my head.

I took another look through the window in the door. There were thirty-three of Stomper Stringfellow's thugs in Jim's Johnasium and — counting Aunt Maud as one and bit — just er . . . two and a bit of us.

"What's the matter, Marlene?" Aunt Maud eyed me quizzically. "You're not nervous, are you?"

"Good heavens, Auntie! Whatever makes you think that? No, I'm not nervous — just dead scared." There was only one thing to do. Quickly I consulted my *Guide for Private Detectives:*

MARLENE MARLOWE'S GUIDE FOR PRIVATE DETECTIVES

3: WHAT TO DO IF YOU'RE DEAD SCARED

1: Shout "Go, Go, Go Geronimo!"
2: Get stuck in.

"Go, Go, Go, Geronimo!" I shouted. But I couldn't move. My feet seemed glued to the floor.

"Er . . . Go, Go, Go," I tried again.

"What are you on about, Marlene?" asked Aunt Maud. "Oh, never mind . . . Come on!" And with that she burst in through the swing doors, dragging me behind her.

CHAPTER 7

As Aunt Maud and I landed in an untidy pile in the middle of the floor, Stomper Stringfellow and his gang stared at us speechless. Then they stared at us rather less than speechless.

"Get hold of those two clowns and do them over. And properly!" roared Stomper Stringfellow.

"Don't worry, Peregrine! Marlene Marlowe's here!" I yelled, running towards the trampoline. Peregrine saw me. Or rather he saw my orange and purple striped face.

"Aaaargh!!!" he screamed at the top of his voice, which was somewhere near the roof.

"Quick! Grab Postlethwaite, grab the pudding, and GO, GO, GO, GERONIMO!" yelled a frenzied Stomper Stringfellow.

His cry brought me up with a start. Stomper Stringfellow must have been reading *Marlene Marlowe's Guide for Private Detectives!* This could mean only one thing — Stomper Stringfellow was not as stupid as he looked. In fact, he was probably more stupid than he looked.

I leapt towards the trampoline to rescue Peregrine, landed on the trampoline and straightaway bounced up to the ceiling . . .

. . . Then bounced back on to the trampoline . . .

Bouncing up towards the ceiling again, I saw Peregrine being hustled out through the doors . . .

. . . On my way down I passed Stomper Stringfellow's smirking features as he stood by the trampoline.

"There's a lot at stake in this game," he snarled. "But you won't get me! I'm warning you, Marlene Marlowe — where we're going, you'd really get the wind up, so don't try and follow. I say! You do look a bit jumpy! Ha Ha!"

"Marlene Marlowe always bounces back," I yelled.

By the time the trampoline stopped there was no sign of Peregrine, Stomper or the gang. I leapt on to a nearby bicycle and pedalled for all I was worth.

As the speedometer passed 50 miles an hour, beads of sweat began to break out on my forehead. Suddenly, I saw Aunt Maud come along beside me.

"What *are* you doing, Marlene?"

"Pedalling for all I'm worth, Auntie!"

"Well, that's about 12½p," replied Aunt Maud. "And, anyway, you'll never catch the gang on that contraption."

"Why not, Auntie?"

"Because it's an exercise bicycle — that's why."

I stopped pedalling and gasped for breath. Aunt Maud was ambling towards the door.

"Right then! That's another successful case completed," she yawned. "I think I'll go home, have a cup of Horlicks and turn in for a good night's sleep," she added.

"But Auntie!" I protested. "You can't! They've still got Peregrine!"

"True. But we've got the Christmas Pudding. Here, catch!"

And it suddenly hit me. Right in the stomach. It was very hard, very large, very black and very round, like a giant cannonball. It was Peregrine's Prize Christmas Pudding all right.

"They left it behind," Aunt Maud explained.

"But I saw them grab it on their way out—"

"That was a medicine ball they picked up by mistake."

"So what are we going to do now?"

"Just stay there and drop everything!" a sinister voice growled from behind us.

We turned round. Facing us was a tall, fair, stony-faced woman in a black, leather jumpsuit. And with her were two heavy looking men and an even heavier looking dog.

I stood still and dropped the pudding. It landed on the stony-faced woman's foot.

"Ye-o-o-w-w-w!!!" she yeowwed.

"Please, Miss, can we have our ball back please?" I asked a little nervously.

One of the heavies rolled the pudding to my feet.

"Well, you did say drop everything," I tried to explain.

"Silence! You talk too much!" bellowed the stony-faced woman.

"I quite agree with you," chipped in Aunt Maud. "She's always been a chatterbox, ever since she was a baby."

The stony-faced woman ignored her. "Now," she said, "which one of you is Stomper Stringfellow?"

I looked at Aunt Maud. Aunt Maud looked back.

"You with the orange and purple face. Come out

here."

"I think she means you, Marlene," Aunt Maud whispered under her breath.

I took ten paces forward. The stony-faced woman thrust a plastic identity card in my face. I took eleven paces back.

"I'm from Puddlethorpe-on-Sea CID," the woman said. "Inspector Grey's the name. Inspector May Grey."

She turned to her colleagues. "And this is Police Sergeant Long, Police Constable Short and Police Dog Bonzo."

"Hi!" I said, handing her my Private Detective's Licence papers. "My name's Marlowe. Marlene Marlowe."

Inspector May Grey studied the papers and then looked up sharply at me. "Not according to these, you're not," she said.

"What!" I exclaimed.

"According to these papers," Inspector May Grey continued, "your real name's Fred Stringfellow, you've got two eyes and your favourite food is lightly poached frog's spawn." I'd given the Inspector my C*O*M*P*U*T*E*R*F*A*X file on Fred "Stomper" Stringfellow by mistake!

"You've got some questions to answer, Stringfellow!" Inspector May Grey went on. "Like why have you stolen Postlethwaite's Prize Christmas Pudding? What exactly is your evil plan? And who's in it with you?"

"Pass," I said. I had no idea how I was going to get out of this one. It looked very much as if I was going to be sent down for ten years for impersonating a villainous villain.

I could hear a loud and frantic knocking coming from below. I looked down. It was my knees.

HOW CAN AUNT MAUD AND MARLENE PROVE THAT MARLENE **IS** MARLENE MARLOWE AND NOT STOMPER STRINGFELLOW? HAVE YOU ANY IDEAS? IF YOU HAVE, WRITE THEM DOWN HERE...

CHAPTER 8

"OK, you two. Start talking," said Inspector May Grey, peering at me with her steely eyes. She looked at Aunt Maud.

"You first."

"Poppycock!" said Aunt Maud.

"Is that Miss, Mrs or Ms?" asked Police Constable Short, who was taking notes.

"I mean poppycock, balderdash and codswallop!" Aunt Maud was furious. "How can this be Fred Stringfellow? Fred's a man's name."

"Frederick is, but Freda's not," retorted the Inspector.

"Inspector, this is Marlene Marlowe. I should know — she's my niece!"

"I've not got time to listen to your personal problems," the Inspector replied airily.

"I can prove it," said Aunt Maud.

"No, Auntie! Don't!" I stared in horror at Aunt Maud, My own Auntie was about to reveal to this awful police officer the exact nature and location of my birthmark. I pulled my bright blue blazer down over my knees. "No, Auntie! You can't. It's private!"

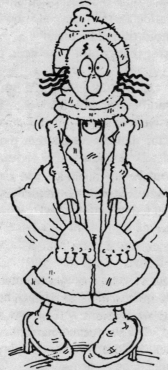

"Silence!" bellowed Inspector May Grey.

"Yes, shut up Marlene!" said Aunt Maud. "How would you describe Fred 'Stomper' Stringfellow?" she asked the Inspector.

Inspector May Grey thought for a moment. "The most calculating, clever and cunning confidence trickster I know."

"Now look at her face," Aunt Maud pointed to me. "She got those orange and purple streaks by getting her new balaclava wet and letting the dye run down her face. Would the most calculating, cunning and clever confidence trickster you know be capable of doing a stupid thing like that?"

The Inspector thought for a moment, then shook her head.

"Exactly," said Aunt Maud. "But Marlene Marlowe, Puddlethorpe-on-Sea's greatest ever Private Detective would."

The Inspector thought for another moment, and nodded her head. "I guess you're right. OK, Miss Marlene Marlowe — you can go. But I'm warning you, stay out of this. Stomper Stringfellow is ruthless and dangerous. I don't know exactly what his game is, but it's big. And if you want my advice, keep out of it."

"But—" I began.

"It's way out of your league, sunshine!" said the Inspector, eye-balling me, "so go back home, make yourself a cup of Horlicks and turn in for a good night's sleep." And she turned on her heel and left, followed by Police Constable Short, Police Sergeant Long and Police Dog Bonzo.

"Oh, well! You heard what the Inspector said, Auntie. You're right. We might as well go home and have a cup of Horlicks."

"What! After what she said? Marlene, I'm surprised you can even suggest such a thing!"

"But it was your idea in the first—"

"There's only one thing you can do with a

42

mystery, Marlene, and that's solve it," said a furious Aunt Maud. "Stomper Stringfellow's racket is obviously even more deadly and dangerous than I thought."

"Well, where do we begin?" I asked Aunt Maud.

"Search me," said Aunt Maud.

I started looking through her pockets. Aunt Maud had obviously been reading her copy of *Marlene Marlowe's Guide for Private Detectives*.

MARLENE MARLOWE'S GUIDE FOR PRIVATE DETECTIVES

4: ESSENTIAL TOOLS OF THE TRADE

1: *A nail file*: Always keep your nails in a file, otherwise they could get lost.

2: *A safety pin*: This can put through your nose, so that you can instantly disguise yourself as a punk.

3: *A lump of chewing gum*: This has many uses, chewing and . . . chewing.

4: *A spare pair of false teeth*: So that if a villain goes through your pockets, they will get their fingers bitten.

All I could find was a nail file, a safety pin, a lump of chewing gum and a spare pair of false teeth.

"Yelp!" I said, as the spare pair of false teeth bit me.

"Marlene," mused Aunt Maud. "What was the last thing Stomper Stringfellow said to you?"

"Er . . . Um . . . " I thought hard.

"Really? Er, Um. Must be a code."

"No, Auntie. I was trying to think. Yes . . . he said 'there's a lot at stake in this game but you won't get me I'm warning you Marlene Marlowe where we're going you'd really get the wind up so don't try and follow.' That was it."

"Mmmm," said Aunt Maud. "There's something missing from what you've just said."

"Is there?"

"Yes. Punctuation. But, it *is* a clue to where they've taken Peregrine."

"Of course! A clue!"

"There's only one problem," continued Aunt Maud.

"What's that, Auntie?"

"We don't know what the clue is."

WHAT IS THE CLUE IN STOMPER STRINGFELLOW'S WORDS? WHERE DO YOU THINK HE HAS TAKEN PEREGRINE POSTLETHWAITE?

CHAPTER 9

"Now, where do you get the wind up, Marlene?" asked Aunt Maud.

"Up through my tummy, into my throat and out—"

"No, Marlene, you indescribable drip! Something that has the name 'wind' in it—"

"Windbag!" I exclaimed.

"Why, you young monkey!" Aunt Maud hit me over the head with her umbrella.

"No, Auntie, I didn't mean you . . . "

"No one insults me like that and gets away with it!" Aunt Maud was waving her arms about excitedly, like an old windmill . . . A windmill!

"A windmill!" I cried. "They've gone to the Old Windmill!"

Aunt Maud thought for a moment. Then she thought for another moment.

"Well, come on then, Marlene! What are we waiting for! Let's get after them!" She charged out through the swing doors and I followed close on her heels. Too close on her heels. I'd just got through the swing doors when they decided to swing back on my behind.

"YEOOW!!!"

I was really fired up. Now I'd got three reasons for wanting Stomper Stringfellow. First, to find out what evil treachery he was up to; second, to get Peregrine, and third, to pay him back for what his swing doors had just done to me.

Aunt Maud and I sat in silence as we drove at

46

speed through the deserted back streets and out of the town towards the Old Windmill that stood on the hills behind Puddlethorpe-on-Sea. Soon the unmistakable scent of the countryside filled my nostrils. I ventured to break the silence.

"Pooh! You always get that rotten old pong when you come out into the country, don't you, Auntie?"

She was sitting with Peregrine's Prize Christmas Pudding between her ankles. "I don't think it's the country that pongs," she answered. She opened her handbag and took out a smelly, bright green sock.

"An interesting piece of evidence this, Marlene. A very interesting piece of evidence. I picked it up in Jim's Johnasium. And the more I think about it, the more I think that it's dead fishy."

"It certainly smells like a dead fishy," I agreed, screwing up my nose. Then something near the top of the sock caught my eye.

"Look! There's a torn name tab here. With the letters 'FC' on it."

"I wonder what 'FC' stands for?"

"Fiona Chadwick!" I instantly replied.

"Fiona Chadwick?"

"Yes . . . _Fiona _Chadwick — FC."

"Er . . . Marlene . . . who exactly *is* Fiona Chadwick?" Aunt Maud had a point. Who *was* Fiona Chadwick?

"Well, I don't actually know anyone called Fiona Chadwick . . . "

"Are you telling me, Marlene, that Fiona Chadwick isn't a real person?"

"No. I mean it stands to reason that there's

somebody somewhere in the world called Fiona Chadwick. And that being so, this could well be her smelly, green sock."

Aunt Maud shut her eyes. "One thing's for certain," she said. "This name tag's like your brain, Marlene — there's a large bit missing."

By now we could see the Old Windmill on top of the hill. I changed down into first gear and we started our ascent. Aunt Maud tapped me on the shoulder. Her lips were moving. I knew this could mean only one of two things: either she was practising ventriloquism or she was trying to tell me something above the roar of the engine. She put her mouth to my ear.

"Marlene, don't you think they'll hear us coming?"

"Not if you keep quiet, Auntie."

"I mean the engine, Marlene!" Aunt Maud had a point. In first gear, the Marlenemobile does sound rather like a demented cat that's got stuck in a spin dryer.

"No problem, Auntie," I smiled. I turned the engine off. "We can coast the rest of the way."

And apart from the occasional crunching sound as Aunt Maud got her false teeth around her chewing-gum, the rest was silence.

Suddenly, as I looked at the windmill, I became aware of something strange and eerie happening. It was very, very frightening.

"A-A-Auntie! L-L-L-Look!" I s-s-s-stuttered. The windmill! It's shrinking!"

"I can't see any windmill . . . "

"That's because it's shrinking!"

"No, that's because I've still got my reading glasses on." Aunt Maud changed her glasses. Then she stared ahead at the windmill.

"It's not the windmill that's shrinking, Marlene Marlowe — it's your brain!"

"My what, Auntie?"

"Did you switch the engine off?"

"Yes, Auntie."

"On top of the hill?"

"Yes, Auntie. So that we could coast the rest of the way.

"Oh, we're coasting, all right.

We're coasting back *down* the hill!"

Aunt Maud was right. Trees were flashing past the window going the wrong way. And the windmill was now a mere speck on the hilltop.

"For goodness' sake, Marlene, pull the handbrake on!"

I grabbed the handbrake. Hard. "Oh no, Auntie!"

"Marlene! You hamfisted head-case! I said pull the handbrake on, not pull it *off*!"

I sat staring at the handbrake in my hand. The Marlenemobile was rapidly gathering speed.

"You know what's at the bottom of the hill, don't you, Marlene?" Aunt Maud was saying, her eyes shut tight.

"No, I was too busy driving to notice when we came up."

I looked back over my shoulder. And shuddered. Yes, it was all coming back to me now. And rather too quickly for my liking. The solid brick wall that ran round Puddlethorpe Park Estate. In a desperate situation like this there was only one thing to do. Consult my copy of *Marlene Marlowe's Guide for Private Detectives*. I looked up "G" for "Going-Backwards-Down-A-Hill-With-The-Engine-Off-nd-No-Brakes" and this is what it said:

MARLENE MARLOWE'S GUIDE FOR PRIVATE DETECTIVES

6: GOING-BACKWARDS-DOWN-A-HILL-WITH-THE-ENGINE-OFF-AND-NO-BRAKES

1:     Don't

There was no doubt about it. The career of Marlene Marlowe, Private Detective, was going very rapidly downhill. And this time I was really coming up against a brick wall. Yes, unless I could think of a way to stop the Marlenemobile, I would very soon be Ex-Private Detective Marlene Marlowe.

HOW CAN MARLENE — OR AUNT MAUD — STOP THE MARLENEMOBILE FROM CRASHING INTO THE BRICK WALL?

AND COME TO THINK OF IT: WHAT DO THE LETTE "FC" ON THE SMELLY GREEN SOCK STAND FOR

AND WHAT DOES STOMPER STRINGFELLOW WAN WITH PEREGRINE POSTLETHWAITE'S PRIZE CHRISTMAS PUDDING?

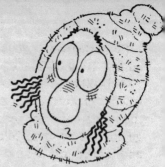

CHAPTER 10

It was true that I was known as the Private Detective who stopped at nothing, but this was ridiculous.

"Ooooh, Auntie! My legs are all wobbly."

"Yes, and you knees are all knobbly. And your face is the colour of this smelly, green sock."

"That's because I feel sick, Auntie . . ."

"There's only one thing that can stop us now. We need to try and jam something hard and solid under the back wheels."

"Ooooh, Auntie, my head!"

"No, that won't do. It's very soft and completely empty. I know! The Christmas Pudding!"

Aunt Maud shoved the Christmas Pudding in the smelly, green sock, opened the sunroof and swung the sock around her head like a catapult. The she let go and the pudding-filled-sock flew through the air and landed just behind the Marlenemobile, so that when we rolled backwards over it—

EEEEEEEICHHHH!

—it jammed under the rear axle, bringing us to a sudden halt.

"Aaaargh!" cried Aunt Maud, as the force of the impact shot her upwards through the sunroof and on to the road below.

I jumped out of the Marlenemobile and dashed over to where she

lay on the ground.

"Well done, Auntie!"

"Eh?"

"You've really managed to flatten out those bumps in the road."

Aunt Maud dusted herself down. "There's only one way we can creep up on the windmill without being noticed, Marlene. We'll have to walk. We can leave the pudding under the Marlenemobile. No one will find it there. Let's go then, Marlene!"

"That's certainly some pudding!" I said. "It's as strong as a football."

Aunt Maud looked at me. "What's that you've just said, Marlene?"

"Er . . . " I thought. "Ummm . . . Oh yes, something about a football."

"Football. FC! Football Club. The smelly, green sock is a football sock!"

"Of course!"

"And I know of only one Football Club whose players wear bright green socks."

"Which one's that, Auntie?"

"Cockleton Colts."

Cockleton was a small town just along the coast from Puddlethorpe. In fact, it was the town where Stomper Stringfellow and his gang all lived. Cockleton Colts Football Club always played in green. It matched the colour of their pitch.

"But what have Cockleton Colts Football Club got to do with Peregrine Postlethwaite's Prize Christmas Pudding?"

"I don't know, Marlene. But the last time I saw

Cockleton Colts in a match, the whole team played like a load of puddings."

We had reached the top of the hill. Before us the dark form of the white, weather-boarded windmill stood out against the sky. Its sails shuddered and squeaked eerily in the breeze. I looked about me carefully, my trained Private Detective's eye taking in all the details of our surroundings. I stiffened. Something told me we were in danger. It was the large sign in front of us that read:

Danger!!!!
Keep Out!!

"Hmmm," said Aunt Maud. "You'd have to be either very brave or very stupid to ignore a notice like that."

"Yes," I agreed.

"Well, I'm very brave."

"Are you, Auntie?"

"Oh, yes. And you, Marlene, are very stupid. So that's all right. Let's go."

"Er . . . Go, go, Geronimo!" I added.

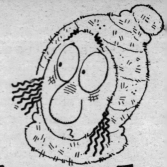

CHAPTER 11

There was a flight of wooden steps leading up to the door of the windmill.

"Goodness, these steps are really old and creaky."

"That's not the steps creaking," replied Aunt Maud. "That's my knees."

We reached the top of the steps. I opened the creaky door to the windmill and peered inside. It was pitch black.

"O-o-o-o-h . . . A-a-auntie . . . "

"Be quiet, Marlene! I think I can hear some people chattering."

"I d-d-don't th-th-think it's some people chattering, Auntie. I think it's my t-t-teeth ch-ch-chattering."

We crept forward into the gloom, one step at a time. Suddenly Aunt Maud struck something. It was a match.

"Ah, that's better. We can see where we are now."

"I know where we are, Auntie. We're in the Old

Windmill on the hill."

"Stop prattling, Marlene, and get up those stairs. Here, take the match."

"Yeowww!"

"Not the lighted end! Never mind, I'll follow the glow of your brilliant fluorescent black braces."

Up the stairs we went. On the next floor a shaft of pale moonlight shone through a window, lighting up the musty room.

"Well, bless my bright blue bloomers!" exclaimed Aunt Maud. There in front of us, bound and gagged, was none other than Peregrine Postlethwaite, Purveyor of the Most Perfect Pastry, Pudding and Profiteroles in Puddlethorpe. We ran over to him.

"Peregrine! Are you all right?" I asked.

"MBUBBURUMPH!" said Peregrine.

"Get the gag off him, Marlene!" Aunt Maud cried.

I ripped the huge piece of elastoplast off his mouth.

"Eeaeaeaiik!" yelled Peregrine.

And I suddenly caught sight of something which made me step back in alarm —

"Aaaargh!!!"

Right on to Aunt Maud's big toe.

"Sorry, Auntie. But this isn't Peregrine Postlethwaite! Peregrine Postlethwaite's got a funny little ginger moustache," I explained.

"I *am* Peregrine Postlethwaite and I have got a funny little ginger moustache," claimed the body on the floor. His squeaky voice sounded like a piece of old chalk being scraped across a blackboard.

"I can't see it," I said.

"That's because you ripped it off when you pulled off my gag. It's on the back of that giant elastoplast."

And so it was.

"Now get those ropes off my wrists and ankles!"

Quickly I untied two clove hitches, three sheepshanks and thirteen granny knots from around Peregrine's ankles. He got up and—

THUD.

Immediately he fell over flat on his face.

"You blundering barmpot, Marlene!" said Aunt Maud, "You've undone his shoelaces instead of the ropes!"

"Do you want these?" I asked Peregrine, scooping up his front teeth from the floor.

"Yesh pleash," said Peregrine.

"I'd lend you my spare false pair, but I've left them back in the Marlenemobile," Aunt Maud added.

We finally got Peregrine unbound. Now at last I could find out the answer to the mystery that had been puzzling me for so long.

"Right!" I began. "There's a question I'd like to ask you that's been bothering me for some time."

"Oh yesh?" Peregrine enquired meekly.

"Yes. Tell me, Peregrine Postlethwaite, how come you've got such a stupid name?" Peregrine opened his mouth to speak. Then Aunt Maud chimed in.

"More to the point, Postlethwaite, you can tell us why Stomper Stringfellow and his gang are so interested in your Prize Christmas Pudding." Peregrine opened his mouth to speak.

59

"And what's it got to do with Cockleton Colts Football Club?" Aunt Maud added.

Peregrine opened his mouth to speak, again. He looked from Aunt Maud to me and back again.

"Come to the top of the windmillsh and I'll show yoush," he said.

"You go, Marlene. I can't be bothered with any more blessed stairs," said Aunt Maud.

I followed Peregrine up three more flights of stairs to the top of the windmill.

"Well?" I asked Peregrine.

I turned to see an evil smile spread across his face as he bared his gums at me.

"Take a look out there, Marlene Marlowe! There'sh the anshwer you're looking for."

I peered out into the murky gloom to where the large wooden arms of the windmill were being lashed by driving icy wind and rain.

Suddenly I felt myself being pushed from behind. As I fell from the top of the mill . . .

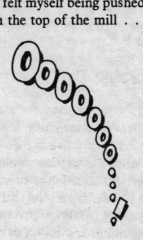

. . . I managed to grab one of the arms just in time.

"He-e-e-l-l-p-p-p!!!" I called.

I heard Peregrine's voice fading into the distance.

"That's your answer, Marlene Marlowe. Just stop trying to interfere in things that don't concern you. You're no match for us!"

The arms of the Old Windmill started to turn. First slowly, then more and more quickly.

. . . I cried.

But there was no one to hear. The nearest I could get to the ground was five metres — far too far to jump. The wind was getting stronger and the rain drove harder. All that I had to save me were the clothes that I wore. It seemed that in this case, the career of Marlene Marlowe, Private Detective, was simply going round and round in circles!

HOW CAN MARLENE ESCAPE FROM THE WINDMILL?

AND WHY IS THE CHRISTMAS PUDDING SO IMPORTANT?

AND WHAT'S IT ALL GOT TO DO WITH THE COCKETON COLTS FOOTBALL CLUB?

JUST WHAT IS STOMPER STRINGFELLOW UP TO?

AND HOW IS PEREGRINE POSTLETHWAITE INVOLVED?

CHAPTER 12

I hung on like grim death to the cold, wet arm of the windmill. With each passing second my hands slipped a little more. My whole life flashed before my eyes, then it flashed down my face and up my nose.

PING!

"ATCHOO!!!" I sneezed, almost letting go of the windmill.

I looked at the clothes I was wearing. My baggy burgundy pants, my bright blue blazer, my brilliant black braces, my big brown boots and my purple and orange balaclava. How could they help to save me?

My hands slipped some more and I braced myself for a long fall to earth — Braces! Of course! Quickly I hooked my brilliant black braces over the arm of the windmill with one hand and then as I swung round to the nearest point to the ground, I let go of the arm of the windmill with my other . . .

I was now bouncing by my braces just six feet away from the ground. I could feel the elastic stretching. I flicked the ends of my braces off their buttons on the top of my trousers and jumped—

"Go, go, go, Geronnnnnn!!!"

Suddenly I heard the sound of a sickening thud and an anguished cry.

"Aaaargh!"

It was me, hitting the ground. Hard. I sat up and flexed my muscles. There was no time to lose. I had

to find Aunt Maud! I leapt up and started to run for all I was worth.

Suddenly I heard once more the sound of a sickening thud and an anguished cry.

"Aaaargh!"

It was me, hitting the ground, again. Even harder.

My baggy burgundy trousers had dropped to my ankles and I'd fallen flat on my face. In a puddle. I'd forgotten that I'd left my brilliant black braces on top of the windmill.

I staggered to my feet and, holding my baggy burgundy trousers up with my hand, clambered up the steps and into the windmill to look for Aunt Maud.

As I reached the first floor, I heard a strange, desperate noise. My sharp Private Detective's brain recognized it immediately. It was the rough, coarse, spluttering sound of an aircraft engine. Somewhere close by, in the dark and stormy sky, there was an ancient biplane in trouble. It sounded very close indeed, close enough to career out of control into the windmill. I threw myself on the floor and waited for the crash.

It didn't come.

But strangely, I could still hear the desperate wheezing and spluttering. It was so loud and close, it sounded as if it were in the room with me. I peeped up out of the corner of my eye. It *was* in the same room as me! Only it wasn't the ancient wreck of a biplane with engine trouble — it was the ancient wreck of Aunt Maud sound asleep and snoring her head off.

"AUNTIE!!!"

"Oooo, who's that? Is it you, Henrykins my darling?"

"It's me! Marlene!" I exclaimed.

"Oh . . . Marlene . . . There's no need to shout."

"I'm not shouting, I'm exclaiming!" I exclaimed.

"Well, it's very loud exclaiming," Aunt Maud stretched and yawned.

"Auntie, how can you go to sleep at a time like this?"

"Easy, I just curl up in a corner, shut my eyes and bisto—"

"Auntie, I've been hanging from the sail of the windmill by my brilliant black braces."

"Marlene, honestly, have you no respect for your clothes? You know how much those braces cost!"

"I didn't do it for fun! I was pushed. By Peregrine Postlethwaite."

"You let that puny little weed push you out of the windmill? Marlene, I'm disappointed in you."

"How was I to know he was a villain, Auntie? I thought he was on our side," I explained, hitching my baggy burgundy trousers up again.

"Come here," said Aunt Maud. "I've got something here in my Private Detective's kit to hold your trousers up."

"Not your spare pair of false teeth?" I said in alarm.

"No, you dafthead! This safety pin." I tied my trousers up with the safety pin.

"Right, Auntie. There's no time to lose if we're

going to catch Peregrine."

I dashed out of the mill and Aunt Maud clattered along behind me. Together we ran back down the hill towards the Marlenemobile. The pudding had gone! Peregrine had obviously taken it when he ran off!

The storm was beginning to lift a little and I looked up along the road back to Puddlethorpe.

"Auntie! There's Peregrine! Running away for all he's worth! See, he's not got very far after all—"

Aunt Maud strained her eyes into the distance. "He is running for all he's worth all right. But he's not running away — he's running towards us!"

"And, oh look, Auntie — all those pretty flashing blue lights following him. It must be a fair."

"Fair? Marlene Marlowe, you feather-brained fathead, they're police cars! Quick!"

There was nothing for it but to roll under the Marlenemobile.

And wait.

67

CHAPTER 13

Screeching squad cars and a panting Peregrine Postlethwaite surrounded the Marlenemobile. I heard car doors slam and peeped out from underneath to see lots of ankles.

"Well, this is her car," I heard a voice saying. A voice I recognized as belonging to Inspector May Grey of Puddlethorpe CID.

"This is where I found my pudding. That horrid

Marlene Marlowe stole it and put it under the back wheels of the car," Peregrine was whining.

"Don't you worry, Mr Postlethwaite, sir," Inspector May Grey replied. "We'll catch her, and when we do, it'll be five years behind bars for her." I shivered.

"And so you'd better!" Peregrine added. "I'm a very important personage in this area."

". . . Purveyor of the most Perfect Puddings, Pastries and Profiteroles, yes sir, I know—"

"And I've also recently become chairman of Cockleton Colts Football Club."

"Really, sir? Congratulations!"

I caught my breath. And Aunt Maud caught hers, too.

"We're in the Cup Final tomorrow against our big rivals Puddlethorpe Juniors. We can't afford to have Marlene Marlowe on the loose while that's going on."

"Don't you worry, sir. We'll get her," intoned Inspector May Grey.

"Oh, and one other thing," squealed Peregrine. "Watch out for the batty old bag who goes round with her."

Quickly, I clapped my hand over Aunt Maud's mouth.

"We will, Mr Postlethwaite. OK, sergeant! Get up to the mill. They can't have gone far."

I saw the ankles disappear, heard the car doors slam, and listened as the police cars roared up the hill towards the mill. I took my hand away from Aunt Maud's mouth.

"Did you hear what he said, Marlene?"

"Yes, Auntie. He said you were a batty old bag."

"Not that, you total twittering twit! He said he was Chairman of Cockleton Colts Football Club. That explains the presence of the smelly, green sock. It suggests that whatever racket Stomper Stringfellow and Postlethwaite are involved in has to do with the Cup Final tomorrow!"

"If that's the case, Auntie, it can't be a racket. You don't use rackets in football. Only tennis."

"Marlene! Of all the stupefying stupidity!"

"Oh, and badminton and squash as well."

"What a drip!" she said.

"Where, Auntie?"

"Coming down from the Marlenemobile's leaking gasket."

I looked up. SPLAT. A large dollop of thick black oil landed in my eye.

"Now you've got a black splodge to match the orange and purple stripes," said Aunt Maud. "Come on, let's get out of here while they're all busy at the mill."

We rolled out from under the Marlenemobile, dusted ourselves down and headed back through the dark, unwelcoming night towards Puddlethorpe.

"Well, there's not a lot more we can do tonight," Aunt Maud said. "We'd best lie low for a bit and make a start early in the morning."

"You're probably right, Auntie. What with Stomper Stringfellow's gang on the look-out for us—"

"And the police. You don't want to be spending

the next five years behind bars, Marlene."

"Oh, I don't know, Auntie. I've always fancied running a pub."

I dropped Aunt Maud off at her place and drove on till I reached a small wooded copse. I drove the Marlenemobile in amongst the trees and turned the engine off. I wasn't risking going back to the flat, just in case Inspector May Grey or Stomper Stringfellow came snooping.

I curled up on the back seat of the Marlenemobile. Bright vivid pictures of the night's events raced through my mind. Suddenly, I felt something sharp and pointed being pressed hard into my stomach.

"Yeooowww!"

I took the safety pin off my baggy burgundy trousers. And curled up again. I took my notebook and wrote down the following. Then I closed my eyes.

FOOTBALL CONNECTION.

PEREGRINE POSTLETHWAITE AND STOMPER STRINGFELLOW ARE IN LEAGUE TO DO SOME NASTY BUSINESS AT THE BIG MATCH.

BUT

WHAT?????

HOW IS THE PRIZE CHRISTMAS PUDDING INVOLVED??????

IF YOU HAVE ANY IDEAS TO HELP MARLENE OUT, THEN WRITE THEM DOWN HERE...

CHAPTER 14

"Dogfish!" exclaimed Aunt Maud.

"I'd prefer cornflakes if it's all the same with you, Auntie," I said in alarm. I'd gone round to Aunt Maud's for an early breakfast, before we set off again on the track of Stomper Stringfellow and his gang.

"Kenny Dogfish! You footballing fat-head!"

"Oh, *that* Dogfish." Kenny Dogfish was Puddlethorpe Junior Football Club's manager.

"Yes. We need to warn him that Stomper Stringfellow and Peregrine Postlethwaite are planning something evil. We'll have a quick, light breakfast."

I gulped down half a bowl of cornflakes while Aunt Maud tucked into her sausage, eggs, bacon, tomatoes, mushrooms, fried bread and kidneys (twice); stewed prunes; salted porridge and toast and marmalade (twelve slices).

Suddenly, there was a furious ringing of the door bell. I jumped and a spoonful of cornflakes went up

74

my nose. As my heart beat faster and faster, Aunt Maud looked at me.

"I'll handle this, Marlene," she said. "Alone."

"But Auntie, be careful—"

Before I could stop her, she had gone to the front door. She opened it. A tall, well-built figure faced her.

"Ah," said Aunt Maud. "Two pints of milk, half a dozen eggs and two cartons of goat's yoghurt."

My Private Detective's brain told me this could mean only one thing: the tall, well-built figure was Aunt Maud's milkman.

"Oh," Aunt Maud continued, "I almost forgot. One milk float, please." She paid her bill and the milkman left.

"Auntie," I said, "what do you want a milk float for?"

"To get us to Wobbley Football Stadium, of course." Wobbley Stadium was a sports arena on the road between Cockleton and Puddlethorpe. Every major football match was played there.

"But what's wrong with the Marlenemobile?" I asked.

Aunt Maud gave me a withering look.

"Oh, I see!" Suddenly I had seen. "You think that Inspector May Grey and Stomper Stringfellow will be looking out for the Marlenemobile, so we go in the milk float as a sort of disguise."

"Well, there is that," agreed Aunt Maud. "But there is a more important consideration."

"Oh?"

"We need to get there quickly and a milk float will

go faster than the Marlenemobile."

Wobbley Stadium was empty, eerie and uninviting. A few screwed-up crisp packets and old battered coke cans blew about on the terraces in the early morning breeze.

We climbed some stone steps and went through a door marked "Ociffe." Aunt Maud peered at the sign through her reading glasses.

"You know what this means, Marlene, don't you?"

Quickly I consulted my copy of *The Very Concise Dictionary for Private Detectives*. This is what it said.

> *Ociffe* (n): See *Spoonerism*.

"John Johnson, who runs Jim's Johnasium, obviously owns Wobbley Stadium, too."

Inside the ociffe was a row of filing cabinets and a huge black desk.

"Right," said Aunt Maud. "Let's see if we can find any clues to these questions that are puzzling us, like one — what are Peregrine and Stomper up to?"

"And two — how does it involve the Christmas Pudding?" I added.

"And three," went on Aunt Maud, "who's that coming up the stairs?"

"That is a tricky one," I mused. "Who's that . . . Help!"

"Quick!" whispered Aunt Maud. "Behind the door."

The footsteps stopped right outside the ociffe door.

"Right. Come out. I know you're in there!" called a voice sharply.

I decided we could bluff it out. "Oh no you don't!" I called back, convincingly.

"Marlene! You blithering banana bonce! You've given us away!" Aunt Maud was furious. And not only that, she was very cross.

"I only know one person who's daft enough to fall for that one," said the voice.

The door suddenly swung open—

"Oooofff!!!

—squashing me between it and the wall. I pulled the door-handle out of my mouth and pushed the door away from me. There in front of us stood a majestic figure in a tartan track suit and gold headband.

CHAPTER 15

"Kenny Dogfish, Manager of Puddlethorpe Juniors Football Club!"

"Aye, that's right," said Kenny, in his broad Scots accent. "Marlene Marlowe, Private Detective, I might have guessed." He looked hard at my orange and purple striped and black-spotted face.

"Well, then, I've never seen you looking better."

"Keep the compliments for later, Kenny. We've got some talking to do." Quickly I explained about PeregrinePostlethwaiteStomperStringfellowthe-smellyfootballsocktheOldWindmillandthePrize-ChristmasPudding.

Kenny's face looked drawn and serious.

"The question is this," I concluded. "What are Peregrine Postlethwaite and Stomper Stringfellow up to, and how does it involve the Christmas Pudding?"

"That's *two* questions," snapped Aunt Maud. Maths was never my strong point.

"I think I've a pretty good idea," said Kenny. "And it fills me with terror." He handed me a menu.

I looked at it. "Thanks," I said. "I'll have the tomato soup."

Aunt Maud said, "I'll have the lot."

Kenny sighed. "This is the menu for today's lunch for the two teams. Look at the bottom of the page, there."

So I looked at the bottom of the page there and saw the words:

Menu

CATERING KINDLY
PROVIDED BY
PEREGRINE POSTLETHWAITE
PURVEYOR OF THE FINEST
PASTRIES, PUDDINGS AND
PROFITEROLES IN
PUDDLETHORPE

CATERING KINDLY PROVIDED BY
PEREGRINE POSTLETHWAITE
PURVEYOR OF THE FINEST PASTRIES,
PUDDINGS AND PROFITEROLES
IN PUDDLETHORPE

"You see, the plan's as plain as the nose on your face,' said Kenny.

"Er . . . the nose on my face isn't very plain. It's got orange and purple stripes and black spots," I pointed out.

Kenny sighed again. "Postlethwaite plans to make the Puddlethorpe Juniors team sleepy, overweight and useless by feeding them his Prize Christmas Pudding for lunch."

"That's outrageous!" cried Aunt Maud. "What a waste of a perfectly good pudding!"

Kenny went on, "That way Cockleton Colts will win the Cup. He obviously arranged for his bakery to be robbed so it looked as if he wasn't involved. And got himself tied up to trick you."

"Don't worry, Kenny," I assured him. "Marlene Marlowe won't let Puny Peregrine Postlethwaite get away with this. I'll soon sort him out. He can't be far away, can he?"

"Puny, is he?" a voice squeaked right behind me.

"You bet!'" I said, turning round. "Really thin . . . "

"Better 'really thin' like me, than really thick, like you, Marlene Marlowe."

An ugly sight confronted me. I was looking straight into the face of Peregrine Postlethwaite.

Behind him stood Stomper Stringfellow. And behind Stomper Stringfellow stood two large thugs.

"What shall we do with them?" whined Peregrine.

"Lock them in the cellar until the match is over." Stomper turned to me. "Then we'll give Inspector May Grey a ring and see what she has to say."

Like a lot of cellars, the one at Wobbley Stadium was in the basement. There were no windows. A single electric bulb burned overhead.

"You won't get out," sneered Peregrine Postlethwaite. "The spare key's locked in the safe. In three hours my Prize Christmas Pudding will be churning around in the stomach of every member of Puddlethorpe Juniors Football Club. And my team will win! Hee! Hee!" His manic laughter echoed around the bare walls and he slammed the door shut.

I looked round. The only items of furniture, apart from the safe, were a few old office desks. Without a word Aunt Maud and Kenny started going through the desk drawers. There was no doubt about it — they were looking for something.

"We need a piece of paper with numbers on it," said Aunt Maud.

"I've got an old bus ticket."

"A *particular* piece of paper, Marlene, you pea-brained prisoner! That has the number of the safe's combination lock on it."

"Ah!" said Kenny, waving a piece of paper in the air.

"Ah!" said Aunt Maud, looking at it.

"Ah!" I said, looking at Aunt Maud.

"Code for the Combination Lock", said the piece of paper. It's not often you get a piece of paper that talks.

But there were no numbers on the piece of paper. Only the following words, which Marlene Marlowe, Private Detective, was finding a bit of a riddle.

MY FIRST IS IN **BAKED**, BUT NOT IN **BEANS**
MY SECOND'S IN **SPRING**, BUT NOT IN **GREENS**
MY THIRD IS IN **STOMACH** AND ALSO IN **ACHE**
MY FOURTH IS IN **CREAM** AND ALSO IN **CAKE**
MY WHOLE IS SOMETHING THAT YOU MUST THROW
AS PART OF THE GAME, WHEN IT COMES TO YOUR GO.
ADD UP THE NUMBERS ON EVERY FACE
AND YOU'LL HAVE THE KEY TO GET OUT OF THIS PLACE

CAN YOU WORK OUT THE ANSWER TO THE RIDDLE?

CHAPTER 16

Aunt Maud took charge of the desperate situation we were in.

"If we're to get out of here in time to save the pudding—"

"And the match," interrupted Kenny.

"And me from Inspector May Grey," I added.

"If we're to get out of here," Aunt Maud repeated, "we must all put our thinking caps on."

"But I've only got my balaclava, Auntie," I protested.

"You infuriating imbecile, Marlene! Just shut up and try to work the riddle out!"

Precious minutes ticked by. Then suddenly everything became clear to me.

"Got it!" I yelled. "The word's DIAC!"

Kenny frowned. Aunt Maud sighed. "I don't think so, Marlene . . . " said Aunt Maud.

"Its fits," I insisted. Look, 'D' is in BAKED but not in BEANS—"

"And brains are in my head, but not in yours, Marlene."

Quickly I looked "diac" up in my copy of *The Very Concise Dictionary for Private Detectives*. This is what is said:

diac (n):   This is not a word.

"Er . . . 'diac' isn't a word," I said, quietly.

"No, but DICE is," said Aunt Maud triumphantly.

"Of course." I saw it all now. "Now why didn't I think of that?"

"Do you really want me to tell you?"

asked Aunt Maud.

"Got any dice on you?" asked Kenny.

"No, but all we need to do is to add up the numbers you get on dice — 1, 2, 3, 4, 5 and 6."

I began counting. Then I hit a problem. "Six and five . . . is nine, ten—. I've run out of fingers."

"Then you'll have to use your toes."

The number came to ten fingers, ten toes and a nose. In other words er — twenty-one. Kenny turned the combination lock on the safe to twenty-one. The door swung open.

Inside was the key. We got the cellar door open and dashed up the steps. There was no one around.

"They'll all be at lunch by now," groaned Kenny.

"What does your watch say, Marlene?"

I looked at it carefully. "Er . . . 'Shock-Resistant, Water-Repellent, All-Digital Quartz Chronometer and Wrist Watch. Made in Japan."

"No, Marlene, you idiotic investigator! The time!"

"Oh . . . Two whiskers past Big Ear's nose."

"Don't worry, Kenny. We should just be able to catch them before they start on the pudding. Come on!"

"Where is the Puddlethorpe Junior's team having lunch, Kenny?"

"The most salubrious restaurant in Puddlethorpe. Nothing but the best for my team."

"You mean they're dining at the Puddlethorpe Plaza?"

"No, they're dining at Puddlethorpe Primary School dining-room."

"Well, what are we waiting for?"

"First of all, you have to say 'Go, go, go, Geronimo'," I explained, but Aunt Maud was already sprinting off to Puddlethorpe Primary School, her navy blue mackintosh flapping about her ankles. Kenny Dogfish followed in hot pursuit and, as I didn't have a hot pursuit, I followed in the milk float.

Over bumps and pot-holes I went, round sharp corners and through red traffic lights. As I reached the school gates, I slammed on the brakes. I looked at the crates behind me. Instead of a hundred and fifty-six pints of milk, I now had a hundred and fifty-six pints of milk shake.

On the school gate, I spotted a poster on which was a photograph of a face, a face I knew well, but a face I could not quite put a name to. I racked my Private Detective's brain.

"Look at that, Marlene," said Aunt Maud.

"I am," I said. "The face is familiar, but I can't put a name to it."

"You gormless goon!" said Aunt Maud. She paused. "It's a photo of you, Marlene!"

"Of course, being Puddlethorpe's most famous Private Detective, I'm bound to be something of a local heroine," I explained, modestly.

"That's not a picture of a heroine," said Kenny. "Look at the writing underneath!"

I looked, and this is what it said:

WANTED

FOR: • ATTEMPTED ROBBERY OF A
PRIZE CHRISTMAS PUDDING

• KIDNAPPING

• DROPPING A CHRISTMAS
PUDDING ON A POLICE
OFFICER'S TOE

MARLENE MARLOWE

AKA BRAINLESS NINCOMPOOP, BUFFOON ETC.

HUGE REWARD

CONTACT INSPECTOR MAY GREY, PUDDLETHORPE C.I.D

"You know what that means, Marlene, don't you?" asked Aunt Maud. I looked at her gleaming eyes. "It means I could take you to the police station and get a hugh reward. Enough probably to buy every Christmas Pudding in Peregrine Postlethwaite's bakery."

"Oh, you can't possibly do that!" pleaded Kenny Dogfish.

It was good to know who your friends were.

"Not this morning. We just haven't got time if we're to rescue my football team," he added.

We charged across the playground, catapulted through the main doors and careered along the corridor to the dining-hall.

We stood there open-mouthed. The place was empty. The scene was one of utter devastation. Plates laden with broken turkey bones, lumps of cold gravy, half-chewed bacon rind and soggy brussels sprouts were stacked to the ceiling. Even worse, pudding bowls containing a few uninviting remains of cold custard and Prize Christmas Pudding were strewn across the tables.

We were too late to save the pudding. But were we too late to save the football team?

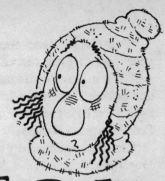

CHAPTER 17

My thoughts were interrupted by a strange sound coming from the kitchens. My Private Detective's brain told me it could be only one of two things: the council refuse cart, churning up a term's worth of school rubbish or Aunt Maud eating. I rushed through to the kitchens.

It was Aunt Maud all right. She was eating her way through a tray of jam doughnuts.

"What are you doing, Auntie?"

"Having lunch, Marlene. Working that blessed riddle out has made me really hungry. And as we were too late to save the pudding . . . "

"Auntie, this is a serious situation! Peregrine Postlethwaite's team are about to pull off the biggest ever swindle in football and win the big match!"

"Not if I have anything to do with it, they're not," said Aunt Maud. And she filled her handbag with all the strawberry doughnuts she had not managed to eat.

Outside, the roads were already full of people and cars going to the big match.

"We'll never get through this lot!" Kenny was panicking. I blew the hooter on the milk float.

"Eeeeek!" it went.

The crowd did not budge. I blew it again. This time it only managed: "Eeee . . . "

"Haven't you got a large, loud hooter?" wailed Kenny.

"No," I said, "but I know someone who has." I turned to look at Aunt Maud and Kenny's eyes followed mine.

"Marlene . . . " Aunt Maud eyed me suspiciously.

"Auntie, you've got to, it's the only way," I pleaded.

"Very well," she agreed. Aunt Maud pulled a large white handkerchief from her sleeve, folded it carefully and blew her nose hard.

"PURRPPP!!!! PURRPPP!!!"

Immediately the crowd scurried into doorways, scarpered round corners and scampered up lamp posts. They looked round about them to try and catch sight of the giant continental juggernaut they had just heard. All they saw was Aunt Maud, blowing her nose and waving at them from the milk float.

"Thank you so much," she called graciously.

Past the crowds we drove, past the steaming hot-dog stalls, past frantic programme sellers, past stands of green and red rosettes. Then all of a sudden it went completely dark.

"Goodness, the days are drawing in," I said. "I didn't realize it was going to be a floodlit match."

"No, Marlene! It's just that I've pulled your balaclava right down over your chin, so that no one can see your face."

"Why have you done that, Auntie?"

"Humanitarian grounds."

I pulled out my copy of *The Very Concise Dictionary for Private Detectives*. But I couldn't see what she meant by "humanitarian". Mainly, because my balaclava was over my eyes.

"There are thousands of people out there waiting to claim a huge reward for handing you over to Inspector May Grey," pointed out Aunt Maud. "It's best that you don't show your face. It could be highly dangerous." The milk float stopped.

"Come on, Marlene," said Aunt Maud.

"Come on, Marlene," said Kenny Dogfish.

They whisked me off my feet and, taking one arm each, carried me into Wobbley Stadium. We seemed to go through an endless number of doors. The dreadful sound of people moaning and groaning caught my ears.

Aunt Maud pulled my balaclava up over my eyes. We were in the Puddlethorpe Juniors dressing room. It was a dreadful sight. Half the team were rolling around clutching their stomachs, while the other half were sound asleep. Peregrine Postlethwaite's Prize Christmas Pudding had certainly done its work.

"Hey, cummon now, lads! Do ye not realize it's the Cup Final?" Kenny was imploring them desperately. He went across to the captain, Larry Twaddle.

"Larry! Say something!"

"Awwwhhh . . ." said Larry Twaddle, suffering from the effects of two extra helpings of Prize Christmas Pudding.

Kenny went across to the striker, Darren Doddle.

"Darren! Say something!"

"Awwwhhh . . ." said Darren. He was still sleeping off the effects of three extra helpings of Prize Christmas Pudding. In fact the Puddlethorpe Juniors teamsheet looked something like this:

PUDDLETHORPE JUNIORS

1:	HARRY TWIDDLE	–ASLEEP
2:	NEV NUTTER	– KEEPS FALLING OVER
3:	LARS-ERIK RASHER*	– KEEPS FALLING OVER NEV NUTTER
4:	BARRY CRUSHER	–ACUTE INDIGESTION
5:	LARRY TWADDLE	–VERY ACUTE INDIGESTION
6:	GARY SMART	–EXTREMELY ACUTE INDIGESTION
7:	GARY BONCE	–SICK
8:	GARY NURDLER	–SNORING
9:	LIAM O'NODD	–ACUTE SNORING
10:	DARREN DODDLE	–ACUTE LITTLE FACE
11:	HENRY LENNY	–CRUCIAL INDIGESTION

MANAGER:
KENNY DOGFISH – FIT AS A FIDDLE

* THE BIG DANISH BACK RASHER

"There's only one thing for it," said Kenny. "I'll have to play the only fit people I've got." He turned round sharply and looked at me.

"What are you like at the back, Marlene?"

"I don't know," I said. "I've never been able to turn my head far enough round to see."

"I mean centre back!" said Kenny in a shrill tone. "And you, Aunt Maud, can you play in goal?"

"In goal?" queried Aunt Maud, thinking hard. "Sounds a blessed funny sort of game to me. Is it like snap?"

"No, it's not a card game, you . . . you . . . ! It's a position on the field! You'd make an excellent goalkeeper."

"I would?" Aunt Maud seemed very pleased.

"Not half," explained Kenny, adding under his breath, "you're twice as big as the goalmouth."

"What's that?" asked Aunt Maud sharply.

"Er . . . I said you're so nice, you're bound to be a big hit in the goalmouth."

"What position will you play, Kenny?" I asked.

"Striker."

"Well, if you're striking, then so am I," said Aunt Maud, stubbornly. "One out, all out. That's my motto."

Kenny was banging his head against the wall. I decided to change the subject.

"I'll need a disguise," I pointed out. "Otherwise I might be recognized. And then I'd be arrested and get myself locked up in prison for five years."

"Promises, promises," sighed Aunt Maud.

"I'll see what's in this cupboard," I said, turning a

handle on the wall. S-P-L-A-S-H-!!! I was soaked through from head to foot. What I had turned on wasn't a cupboard handle, but the changing-room showers.

"Och, just look at that!" said Kenny. "Marlene's decided to disguise herself as a sponge."

"I'm absolutely wet!" I yelled.

"That's the most intelligent thing you've said all day, Marlene," agreed Aunt Maud.

"Look at her face!" Kenny said suddenly.

"Do I have to?" asked Aunt Maud, reluctantly.

"All the orange and purple stripes and the black spots have been washed away!" Kenny continued, excitedly. "Is she nae canny?"

"She's certainly not a bit like the picture on the 'Wanted' posters," agreed Aunt Maud. "That settles it. You can go out disguised as yourself, Marlene."

"There's one other problem," I said.

"Oh aye?" Kenny looked puzzled.

"Yes. There's three of us — and eleven of them."

Aunt Maud smiled to herself. "I've got a little plan up my sleeve. Well, not up my sleeve exactly, more like . . . in my handbag."

"You're never taking that handbag with you on to the pitch?" Kenny looked dumbfounded.

"It's *your* only chance of winning the cup, and *our* only chance of cornering Peregrine Postlethwaite," Aunt Maud insisted.

Kenny, Aunt Maud and I trotted out of the dressing-room and through the players' tunnel. I caught a glimpse of the Cockleton Colts team running on to the pitch. Most of them were members of Stomper Stringfellow's gang. They looked mean, moody and muscular. I gulped and felt very sick indeed. How could Aunt Maud have a plan that would work against this lot?

At that moment, there was only one position I had any desire to play in, and that was right back. Right back behind the goal.

CHAPTER 18

There was a great cheer as we ran on to the rich, green turf of Wobbley Stadium. I immediately did as Kenny had told me and sat down in the middle of the pitch and blew into my hands.

"What are you playing at, Marlene?" Kenny didn't sound too happy.

"Well, you did say to do some warming-up exercises," I protested.

"I meant running on the spot, touching your toes, that sort of thing, you stupid sassenach!"

I tried, but it's very difficult to run on the spot while trying to touch your toes.

The referee blew his whistle and we lined up to be presented to the Mayor. I heard Stomper Stringfellow snigger to Kenny.

"What's up, Dogfish? Only three of your team turn up? Hee! Hee!"

"You won't get away with this, Stringfellow!" Kenny hissed.

"And who's this, Dogfish? A new signing?" Stomper Stringfellow looked straight at me, without realizing who I really was.

"My new centre back," said Kenny.

"Mmmm, she looks like you should've 'sent-her-back' — a very long time ago!" Stomper Stringfellow laughed.

I looked up and caught sight of Peregrine Postlethwaite smirking away in his luxury hospitality suite in the main stand. I just hoped that Aunt Maud's plan was foolproof.

The ref blew his whistle again. The match was underway. And then a funny thing happened.

As soon as any of Stomper Stringfellow's team moved with any speed, they fell over. And if they tried to run, they seemed to have to use very small steps.

Up near the goalmouth, I whispered to Aunt Maud.

"What's happening, Auntie?"

She grinned a wicked grin. "My plan is working! You see, when we were lined up before the Mayor at the start, I managed to slip a sticky jam doughnut between the knees of every Cockleton player! Their knees are stuck together! With any luck we could win this one!"

We did. The final score which flashed up on the scoreboard was:

COCKLETON COLTS: 1
(MARLOWE o.g.)

PUDDLETON
JUNIORS: 52
(DOGFISH 52)

Stomper Stringfellow and Peregrine Postlethwaite's mean plan had been halted at the last moment! The crowd was singing and chanting. But Kenny stood silently in the middle of the pitch.

"Och, it's no good, Marlene. We taught Peregrine Postlethwaite and Stomper Stringfellow a lesson, but we didna win fairly today. I can't take the cup for Puddlethorpe Juniors after a match like that."

"Well, we've got Postlethwaite where we want him," reasoned Aunt Maud. "I'm sure he could be persuaded to play the match again, under proper conditions."

Kenny started on his lap of honour, while Aunt Maud and I went in search of Peregrine Postlethwaite. We found him at the back of the main terrace trying to make good his escape.

"POSTLETHWAITE!" Aunt Maud shouted at him in capital letters. The huge crowd was silent and all eyes turned to us. Aunt Maud lowered her voice until it was in her socks.

"Shall I tell this crowd the truth about your skullduggery, Postlethwaite? Just one word from us about what you've done and they'll put you in the oven along with your puddings."

There was only one thing Peregrine Postlethwaite could say to that. "Can I borrow your *Very Precise Dictionary for Private Detectives*, Marlene?"

He flicked through the pages.

"What does it say, Peregrine?"

"Skullduggery: what evil villains get up to."

So now he knew. And so did I . . .

"We'll make a deal with you, Postlethwaite," Aunt

Maud continued.

By now the crowd had its attention on Kenny's victory run around the pitch.

"We won't tell the crowd what you've been up to—"

"Oh, thank you! Thank you!" the wretched, whingeing young baker whined.

"But there is a price to pay," I said menacingly.

"I'll pay you! Any amount!" Peregrine Postlethwaite was squirming and wringing his hands in terror. Suddenly I saw Aunt Maud's face go a deathly white.

"What's the matter, Auntie?"

"The matter is one of arrest," a voice behind me said. I spun round to come face to face with Inspector May Grey. I breathed a sigh of relief.

"Oh good," I said. I could do with a rest. I've been on the go since breakfast."

"I mean *arrest*, not *a rest*! As in arrest for attempted robbery of a prize Christmas Pudding, kidnapping, dropping a Christmas Pudding on a police officer's toe and now — attempted bribery!"

Aunt Maud spoke. "I think, Inspector, Mr Postlethwaite has something to say on the issue."

"Er . . . that's right," said Peregrine. "I'd like to say that Marlene Marlowe is a very wonderful person," Aunt Maud eyed him fearfully, "and so is her Aunt Maud."

Inspector May Grey looked from Peregrine Postlethwaite to me to Aunt Maud and back again.

"Are you saying you want me to drop all charges?" Peregrine Postlethwaite nodded.

"Are you sure?" Inspector May Grey asked icily.

Aunt Maud gave Peregrine a glance out of the corner of her eye and he nodded again.

"Well, if you say so, Mr Postlethwaite," Inspector May Grey hissed. "But if you ask me, something around here doesn't quite add up."

"That's Marlene's brain," pointed out Aunt Maud.

Inspector May Grey turned on her heels and marched out, still glaring at us with utter contempt.

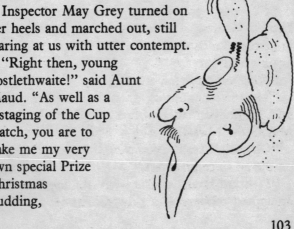

"Right then, young Postlethwaite!" said Aunt Maud. "As well as a restaging of the Cup match, you are to bake me my very own special Prize Christmas Pudding, twice as big as the one you fed to the Puddlethorpe Juniors Football Team."

"Of course, dear lady. It would be a pleasure," squeaked Peregrine Postlethwaite, bowing and scraping. "And what can I bake that would suit Puddlethorpe's greatest ever Private Detective?"

"Something very nutty," said Aunt Maud.

Exactly one week later, Aunt Maud and I sat in Peregrine Postlethwaite's hospitality suite at Wobbley Stadium and watched Puddlethorpe Juniors beat Cockleton Colts 4-2 in the restaged Cup Final. Looking at Peregrine out of the corner of my eye, I still had my doubts about him. He would certainly need to go down in my book of villains.

But really, there was no getting away from it: in the case of Marlene Marlowe and the Great Christmas Pudding Mystery, everything had turned out right as pie.

YOU CAN FILL IN MARLENE'S
C★*O*★*M*★*P*★*U*★*T*★*E*★*R*★*F*★*A*★*X*
DETAILS ON
PEREGRINE POSTLEWAITE . . .

Q

Quite Evil Villains

PEREGRINE POSTLETHWAITE:

REAL NAME:

HEIGHT:

WEIGHT:

EYES:

NOSE:

FAVOURITE
COLOUR:

MOST FAVOURITE
FOOD:

LEAST FAVOURITE
FOOD:

PERSON HE MOST
ADMIRES:

ADDRESS OF
HIDEOUT:

ANY OTHER
RELEVANT INFORMATION

MARLENE MARLOWE INVESTIGATES ·

*My name is Marlene. Marlene Marlowe. And I'm the
dottiest detective ever to have missed a clue . . .*

Follow the hilarious trail of the world's most clueless
private eye in these books by Hippo:

Marlene Marlowe Investigates the Great Christmas Pudding Mystery £1.75

Early one morning Marlene is woken by a phonecall:
"Come to Peregrine Postlethwaite's bakery immediately!"
In the dimly-lit building Marlene follows a trail of dark red
sticky mess, leading to a large moving bundle . . .

Marlene Marlowe Investigates the Missing Tapes Affair £1.75

A phonecall summons Marlene to the house of an old
friend. There, slumped on the kitchen floor, lies the
twisted body of a young man . . .

You'll find these and many more great Hippo books at
your local bookseller, or you can order them direct. Just
send off to *Customer Services, Hippo Books, Westfield
Road, Southam, Leamington Spa, Warwickshire CV33
OJH*, not forgetting to enclose a cheque or postal order
for the price of the book(s) plus 30p per book for postage
and packing.